Lucy ~~and the~~ Bully

Claire Alexander

For Dennis, Christine, Mark, Elsie and Jim . . .
C.A.

Pig
by
Luther

Worm
by
Paula

Monster
by
Martin

Thing
by
Tommy

Crow
by
Lucy

Frog
by
Sophie

First published in Great Britain in 2008 by Gullane Children's Books.
This paperback edition published in 2009 by

Gullane Children's Books

185 Fleet Street, London EC4A 2HS
www.gullanebooks.com

1   3   5   7   9   10   8   6   4   2

Text and illustrations © Claire Alexander 2008

The right of Claire Alexander to be identified as the author and illustrator of
this work has been asserted by her in accordance with the Copyright, Designs and Patents Act, 1988.

A CIP record for this title is available from the British Library.

ISBN-13: 978-1-86233-755-8

Printed and bound in Indonesia

Lucy and the Bully

Claire Alexander

GULLANE
CHILDREN'S BOOKS

In class, everyone asked
Lucy to draw for them . . .

Well, not quite everyone . . .

Tommy got up and went over to Lucy's table.
"Oops, clumsy me," he said, as he pushed over the paint pot.

"Oh dear!" flapped
Miss Goosie the teacher.
"Accidents will happen, let's
get this mess cleared up!"

At Nursery the next day, everyone had to make a model.
Miss Goosie awarded Lucy a gold star for her blackbird . . .

Pig
by
Luther

Worm
by
Paula

Monster
by
Martin

Even though she thought it was a crow.

At home time, Lucy carried
her model very carefully
so it wouldn't break.

But Tommy was waiting . . .

"Let's see your stupid crow, then!" he said.
"Um . . . it's a blackbird," Lucy stammered.
But Tommy wasn't listening, and he . . .

. . . stamped on it.
"Don't tell on me, or else!"
he snorted.

"NO! Please don't do that!"

Lucy put the broken blackbird
into her bag, so her mummy
wouldn't see. And she
didn't say anything.

That night, Lucy tried hard to put her blackbird
back together, but it just didn't look the same.
"What happened to your sculpture?" her mummy asked.
"I - I - I dropped it," said Lucy sadly.

Over the next few days, Lucy's mummy
sensed there was something very wrong.

On Monday,
Lucy brought home
a ripped story book.

On Tuesday,
she brought home
a scrumpled painting,

and on Wednesday,
she brought home pencils
that were broken in two.

Lucy looked sadder and sadder every day,
but she wouldn't tell her mummy why.

On Thursday, Lucy brought home a cake she'd baked. "What's that hoofprint doing in the middle?" asked Mummy. "I-I-I don't know," said Lucy.

But her mother knew there was only one calf in Miss Goosie's class.

Before Lucy could say anything,
her mummy was on the telephone.
"Can I speak to Miss Goosie, please?" she said.
"No, Mummy!" wailed Lucy.
"Please don't tell Miss Goosie!"

But it was too late.

That night, Lucy couldn't sleep
for fear of what might happen the next day.

In the morning, Lucy
didn't want to go inside.
"Don't worry, Miss Goosie
will look after you,"
said her mummy.
"Off you go now."

"Come on you naughty little bull,
Miss Goosie is waiting."

Tommy didn't want
to go inside either.

At story-time Tommy was very quiet.

At playtime Tommy looked
very small and very sad. Lucy
no longer felt scared of him,
in fact she felt sorry for him.

At activity time Lucy saw that Tommy was drawing something.
It was a hedgehog, and it was a very good hedgehog.
Its spikes looked very sharp and spiky indeed.

Lucy decided to tell him exactly
what she thought of it . . .

"I like your hedgehog, Tommy," Lucy said.
"It's not a hedgehog, it's a porcupine," said Tommy.
"Well I like it," said Lucy. "Please will you draw one for me too?"

Tommy was shocked.
No one had asked him to draw anything for them before . . .

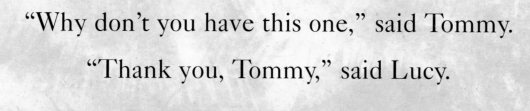

"Why don't you have this one," said Tommy.

"Thank you, Tommy," said Lucy.

"Lucy, I'm sorry I was mean, and did all those things
and most of all I'm sorry I stamped on your crow,"
Tommy said. "It was a very good crow."

"I forgive you, Tommy," said Lucy. "But it wasn't a crow, it was a blackbird."

They both laughed, and went outside to play.